SEREFINA
UNDER THE
CIRCUMSTANCES

by
Phyllis Theroux

pictures by
Marjorie Priceman

GREENWILLOW BOOKS, NEW YORK

For the children of
Charles W. Raymond
Elementary School
in Washington, D.C.

Gouache was used for the full-color art.
The text type is Italia Book.

Text copyright © 1999
by Phyllis Theroux
Illustrations copyright © 1999
by Marjorie Priceman

Printed in Hong Kong by South China
Printing Company (1988) Ltd.

First Edition
10 9 8 7 6 5 4 3 2 1

Library of Congress
Cataloging-in-Publication Data

Theroux, Phyllis.
Serefina under the circumstances /
by Phyllis Theroux ;
illustrated by Marjorie Priceman.
      p.   cm.
Summary: Serefina's imagination
makes her destined for greatness,
according to her grandmother, but
sometimes it leads her into trouble
as well.
ISBN 0-688-15942-7
[1. Imagination—Fiction.
2. Grandmothers—Fiction.
3. Storytelling—Fiction.]
I. Priceman, Marjorie, ill.   II. Title.
PZ7.T35245Se   1999   [Fic]—dc21
98-50915   CIP   AC

Serefina loved her grandmother for two reasons: She told good stories, and she took Serefina seriously.

"I think that you are destined for greatness," Serefina's grandmother told Serefina one night after supper.

Serefina's eyes widened. "How am I destined for greatness, Grandma?"

"Well," her grandmother replied, "that remains
to be seen. But you've got a very good imagination,
which is the main thing. In fact, you come from
a long line of people who are full of imagination."

Serefina saw herself hanging from a long
clothesline with a lot of great-aunts, great-uncles,
and distant cousins she had never met.

"But right now," said her grandmother, "I am
imagining a seven-year-old girl who looks quite
a lot like you getting the dishes washed while
I try to get your brother into bed. He's beside
himself about his birthday tomorrow."

"Will you tell me a story before I go to bed?" Serefina asked.

"If there is time," her grandmother replied.

Serefina rushed through the dishes, brushed her teeth, and got into her nightgown, so that when her grandmother came into her room, she could begin the story right away.

"So," said her grandmother as she settled herself on the edge of Serefina's bed, "what kind of story shall it be tonight?"

"Tell me a story about when you were little and got into trouble," said Serefina.

Her grandmother smiled. "Did I ever get into trouble? Let me refresh my memory."

Serefina thought "refresh my memory" had a cool, iced-tea sound to it. She decided to find a way to use it in school tomorrow.

"Well," said Serefina's grandmother,
"would you like to hear about the time I won
first prize in a rodeo when I was in kindergarten?"

"Grandma," exclaimed Serefina, "I didn't know
you could ride a horse."

"I couldn't," said her grandmother, "but I wished
I could. And one morning when the teacher asked
if anyone in the class had any news for show-and-tell,
I raised my hand and said that I had won first prize,
which was a solid gold saddle, at the Cow
Palace Rodeo."

"Did your teacher believe you?" asked Serefina.

"She acted as if she did," said Serafina's grandmother. "In fact, it was such a good story that I believed it, too. But when my mother came to pick me up after school, the teacher asked her if I could bring the gold saddle to school to show everybody."

"Oh, no!" said Serefina. "What happened then?"

"My mother took me home and made me write a letter to the teacher telling her I had made the whole thing up, and I wasn't allowed to play with any of my friends after school for a whole week—so I would remember not to tell any more tales."

"But it was a very good tale," said Serefina.

Serefina's grandmother smiled. "Yes," she said, "it was. But it didn't happen to be the truth. So you see, Serefina, having an imagination is a blessing unless you let it run away with you."

She took Serefina's face between her long, cool fingers and looked into her eyes. "Do you know what I mean, Serefina?"

"Ummm-hmm," said Serefina, sliding her eyes sideways. She knew what her grandmother meant. But sometimes the truth was so big, like a mountain without a tunnel, that she had to use her imagination to get around it.

Serefina's grandmother stood up and then sat down on the bed again. "Serefina," she said, "can you keep a secret?"

Serefina couldn't believe it. Nobody ever gave her a secret to keep—for one reason. She had never successfully kept one. For Serefina, trying to keep a secret was like trying to drink ginger ale without burping.

"Oh, yes!" Serefina exclaimed.

"I'm going to give Buster a surprise birthday party after school tomorrow, and I need you to take him to the park for about fifteen extra minutes so his friends can get to the house ahead of him. Can I count on you?"

"Up to one million," said Serefina, who liked to be counted on.

"All right, then," said her grandmother. "If I count very slowly, I guess we'll make it. Good night, Serefina."

As Serefina slept, the secret lay like a tiny seed, covered by the warm, dark soil of her dreaming. In fact, when Serefina woke up the next morning, she forgot the secret was even there.

Serefina's grandmother reminded her. "Remember," she whispered into Serefina's ear at breakfast, "to keep your mouth closed about Buster's surprise party."

"I'm locking my lips and throwing away the key, Grandma," Serefina whispered back.

"That's fine," said her grandmother, "as long as you don't go looking for that key in the bushes later on."

The whole way to school Serefina didn't say a word to Buster. Keeping a secret was easier than she had remembered. But it had been such a long time since Serefina had been given a secret to keep that she had forgotten something. A new secret takes time to grow.

As Serefina practiced her double-Dutch jump rope before the bell rang, the secret was no bigger than a sprout. She hardly noticed it.

By the morning spelling bee it was still just a twig of a secret, with a couple of leaves.

"Serefina," called her teacher, Mrs. Otis, "spell 'originality.'"

"O-R-I-G-E-" Serefina began.

"Not quite," said Mrs. Otis. "Never mind, Serefina, it's better to have originality than to know how to spell it. But someday I expect you to have both."

By geography class the secret had grown tall enough so that it brushed against Serefina's shoulder and made it difficult for her to concentrate.

"Serefina," said Mrs. Otis, "I believe you are daydreaming. Can you tell us, please, what is the capital of South Dakota?"

"Could you refresh my memory?" asked Serefina.

"Don't get smart with me," said Mrs. Otis. "I'm looking for Bismark, not RE-marks."

By choir practice the secret
was so large, with so many
branches and such a thick trunk, that
Serefina could hardly read the
words of the songs on the
blackboard.

And by three o'clock when she went to pick Buster up at kindergarten, the secret had gotten so enormous that it was shoving its branches through every window, with roots snaking down staircases and filling up the halls.

The secret was everywhere Serefina looked, except in Buster's eyes, which were full of tears.

"What's the matter?" Serefina asked.

"An ant bit me on the lip when I got a drink at the water fountain," said Buster.

Serefina looked at Buster. Buster began to wail. Serefina hated it when Buster cried, because it always sounded as if he were going to cough his whole heart out onto the sidewalk.

"Quit crying, Buster," she whispered as she grabbed him by the hand and dragged him gurgling out of the school yard. "You're embarrassing me."

But Buster only cried louder.

"I said, quit it," Serefina repeated as she pulled him down the sidewalk toward the park.

But Buster only upgraded his tears to a tantrum and threw himself on the ground.

"Oh, no," said Serefina, who couldn't think of what to do. But just then she saw something glittering in the bushes.

And Serefina used it.

And Buster stopped crying right away.

That evening as her grandmother combed Serefina's hair, Serefina explained why she couldn't keep the secret from Buster.

"I had to tell him, Grandma. You would have told him, too, under the circumstances."

"Serefina," said her grandmother, "you are always under some kind of circumstances."

"But Buster's life was *at stake*!" Serefina insisted.

Serefina had found that expression in a book about a lion tamer in the circus. "All he had, going into the cage," the book had said, "was his whip and his fantastic ability to communicate with the big cats with his eyes. Every night his life was *at stake*."

"Oh, really," said Serafina's grandmother. "How was Buster's life at stake?"

"Balloon lips," said Serefina.

"Balloon what?" exclaimed her grandmother.

"Balloon lips," repeated Serefina, "You can get it from ant bites. I read about it in . . . maybe I only heard about it, but I couldn't take any chances, Grandma, and there was only one way I could think of to snap him out of it.

"And so," Serafina continued, "I said to Buster, 'Now look, I'm not supposed to tell you this, but if you quit crying for a minute, I will tell you a secret.' And Buster quieted down long enough for me to tell him that there was a surprise party for him at home, and if he didn't run fast, he'd miss the whole thing."

Serefina's grandmother stopped combing Serefina's hair and waited for her to finish.

"Grandma, you have no idea how happy I was to see Buster running, a little stiff at first, but still running, and by the time he got home, he was completely cured!"

Serefina's grandmother turned Serefina around
and kissed her on the forehead. "Thank you,
Serefina," she said, "for being you."

"And," she added, as she pulled Serefina onto
her lap, "thank you for telling such a good story."
She looked down into Serefina's eyes. "And thank
you for saving Buster's life."

"Don't mention it," said Serefina, snuggling into
the curve of her grandmother's side. "It was the least
I could do." Every once in a while Serefina got the
chance to use two good expressions at the same time.

That night Serefina dreamed that her grandmother
whispered something wonderful and surprising
into her ear. It was warm and light and floated like
a golden leaf upon the waters of her dreaming.

The next morning Serefina woke up and remembered what it was. She was destined for greatness. Serefina wasn't sure she believed it, but her grandmother did, which was even better.

	DATE DUE		
			•